P9-DNI-289

# Judy Scuppernong

# *Judy Scuppernong*

BRENDA SEABROOKE

*Illustrated by* TED LEWIN

Cobblehill Books • Dutton • New York

Library of Congress Cataloging-in-Publication Data
Seabrooke, Brenda.
Judy Scuppernong / Brenda Seabrooke ; illustrated by Ted Lewin
p. cm.
Summary: Poems decribe the daily experiences of four girls growing up in a small town in Georgia in the early 1950s.
ISBN 0-525-65038-5
1. Girls—Juvenile poetry. 2. Georgia—Juvenile poetry. 3. Children's poetry, American. [1. Friendship—Poetry. 2. American poetry.]
I. Lewin, Ted, ill. II. Title.
PS3569.E154J84 1990 811'.54—dc20 90-31583 CIP AC

Published in the United States by Cobblehill Books, an affiliate of Dutton Children's Books, a division of Penguin Books USA Inc.

Designer: Jean Krulis
Printed in the United States of America
First edition 10 9 8 7 6 5 4 3 2

*To the real Stacy and Lala,*
*Andrea Chalverus Doughtie*
*and Bonnie Peavy Hair*

---

*To Brent Ashabranner—JUDY'S guardian angel*

# From the Grape Arbor

We discussed our lives
that summer from the top
of the grape arbor where
we perched, our legs dangling
while we ate the green
scuppernongs as big as giant marbles,
sucking the sweet pulp, chewing
the thick skin for the last squeeze of
juice before spitting it on the ground
below, already littered with the wrinkled
drying skins of other days.
I'm Norwegian, Judy said.
We'd never met a Norwegian before.
The way she said it made her seem
exotic to us, like one
of those closed shells
from Japan that when
you dropped it into a bowl
of water suddenly
sprouts a bouquet

of flowers. Her long
flaxen hair was cut straight
across and she
had bangs.
We had curls
and braids and ponytails.
Sometimes we hung
upside down from the arbor.

Our braids and curls
and ponytails flapped
the wrong way. Judy's
hair swept the ground.
The world was a different place
from our point of view.
The ground was leafy,
the sky was grass.
When we sat up again
with faces flushed
our old world seemed
somehow new.

# *Judy's House*

We were never allowed
in Judy's house. No reason
was given, no excuse
made, no words spoken.
But we knew
not to go past the back
steps. Beyond, the house was
quiet with dim held breath,
her mother a shadow,
a silhouette two rooms
away, a silent whisper,
behind lowered shades. If
we were thirsty, we drank
from the spigot outside
beneath the kitchen window.
We knew it was
the kitchen because
sometimes we could hear
the faucet dripping
in the sink and the faint

hum of the refrigerator.
Judy lived in a house but
to us it was a cavern, cool
and dark with secrets.

# Lunch

No you may not go to the Spotted Pig
for lunch with Judy. So Judy
went alone, crossing
all those streets
in the hot summer noon, having
an adventure by herself with
the money jingling in her shorts pocket.
We ate our dinners, fried
chicken, pork chops, or ham with
summer vegetables and biscuits
oozing with amberous
preserves and for dessert
a dark swamp of blackberry pie
crisscrossed with pastry paths,
while our mouths dreamed of
Judy and her cheeseburgers and fries.

## The Spotted Pig

It was a famous landmark
on the main highway from the North
to Florida. Strangers would say
Fitzgerald, that's where
the Spotted Pig is. Best
cheeseburgers in the South.
Nowhere else counted.
People came all the way
from Atlanta for the Pig's
cheeseburgers, handmade
patties on buoyant rolls
glued together with slabs
of melted cheese.
We went to the Pig
with our parents who
sat at hard-seated booths
or tables while
we sat on red plastic-cushioned
stools at the counter where
we could watch the owner's

wife, lights leaping in
her spectacles as she fried things
to the tunes of the jukebox, a nickel
each and a show of bubbling rainbow
lights. Big-faced fans
like electric flowers turned
from side to side on long stems,
droning the greased air

over the diners so that
afterwards, if
we were going to church
we had to change our clothes
or everyone would know
we'd just come from
the Spotted Pig and hadn't
eaten warmed-over
Sunday dinner.

# The Baker

The breadman entered
the Spotted Pig through
the side door directly
into the kitchen. He
baked the bread
this morning, kneading
the dough early in long
troughs so it would
rise and be cooked in stone
ovens and ready for sale
before ten.

He had a big voice with
a tiny lisp in the corners. There
were always a lot of jokes
when he came. His bread,
rolls, and cakes were famous, too.
Ball's Bakery ran
Ranger bread out of town.

Barney made all
our birthday cakes, pale
pastel overlaid with lacy
lattice, our names twined
through it like climbing
roses with pink and yellow
buds and tiny green leaves
and sometimes a butterfly
to dot an *i*.

# Judy Alone

We knew our mothers disapproved
of Judy. They never said
so. Looks were enough.
Her mother always stayed
indoors. There was no sign
of a father. Judy Scupholm
was her name but we
called her
Judy Scuppernong.

## *We*

Your names are too long
Judy said. Why
don't you have a nickname
like me?
We looked at each other,
Deanna, Eustacia, and
Laura Louise, we'd
always been, and
that summer became
Stacy and Lala but I
stayed Deanna because
I refused to be Dee.

## The Glasshouse

There was a glasshouse in Judy's backyard. Some of the panes were still in. We went down the stone steps

and sat on a shelf that was below
ground level and thought glass thoughts.
The stone floor was scattered
with broken glass that glimmered
like splashes of water.
It's a greenhouse, Judy
insisted. We didn't see why.
There was nothing green in it.
The glass on the stones
seemed to grow as summer wore
on. Soon we couldn't step
around it and had to wear
shoes when we went in.
But the pecan trees that sheltered
us from the sky made green walls
and a green ceiling through the glass panes.
Maybe that was where the name came from.
Judy's eyes were the same green.

# *Old Mrs. Cole*

Judy's house was owned
by old Mrs. Cole. Mr. Cole
had never married her. A common-
law wife our mothers said. She lived
across the street with her daughter,
Iola, and Iola's husband, Mr. Rawlings.
They were married. Mr. Rawlings
is a good man, our mothers
said. Iola is a . . .
They looked at each other.
We observed Iola. We couldn't see
what she was that others weren't.
She gardened a lot
in a straw sun hat,
her clothes were always floppy
and untidy looking,
but her house was prim and white
and her yard was the neatest
in town. Iola never
went anywhere

without her mother.

We watched old Mrs. Cole
but not too closely
lest she caught us with her eyes.
We didn't want common law.
We discussed the disease.
Could it be like ringworm or cooties?

Old Mrs. Cole always wore
a shapeless brown coat
and a shapeless brown hat pulled
down over her ears. She's bald
said our mothers. But
we couldn't see through the hat.
Maybe she has to shave her head,
we suggested. She had
a wrinkled monkey face
and blackberry eyes
with thorny lashes.
We were scared
to death of her.

The garage behind Judy's house
was filled with Mrs. Cole's things.

Not even Judy was allowed in. But
we went in anyway and found in a box
a wig with long brown
braids. Nobody would even try
it on. We didn't want to catch
Mrs. Cole.

# Chameleons

A green chameleon sleeping
on the stone ledge in
the glasshouse turned
the color of stone. Judy's skin
was as pale as the cream floating
at the top of the milk bottles
left on the front steps cool
with dew every morning at our houses.
Was it because she was Norwegian?
Although she played outside
with us everyday
she lived in that gloomy house.
If she lived in the glasshouse
would her skin turn
translucent or green?

# This and That

Judy calls them polliwogs.
They are tadpoles, we insist.
Our consulted mothers say
they are both. How
can something be both
we wonder. Things have to be
one or the other.
Our mothers smile.
Some people call peanuts
goobers, they say,
and groundnuts,
and goober peas
and pinders
they say.
Judy calls blue jeans
dungarees and rolls them
up to her knees.
We read the funny papers
and funny books but
Judy reads the comics.

She brings ice out
to the backyard and says
she got it out of the refrigerator,
which we know is a Frigidaire.
She volunteers that her mother
calls us youngsters. But
we know that we
are children.

# *Ladies of the Morning*

We wanted to be
glamorous
like movie stars,
to glitter
in sequins and jewels.
So we begged
old nightgowns from our
mothers, painted our faces,
and draped ourselves
with their discarded jewelry.
I slit
my ice-blue satin
almost up to my knee
to show off
my red high heels.
At 6 A.M. we stood,
a bouquet of rose, peach,
and blue on the corner
waiting. Judy came slinking
up in rhinestones and black

lace, the envy of all of us.
We ripped off our
neck ruffles and daringly
I showed my knees,
one purple with a bruised
scrape and the other
crisscrossed with Band-Aids.
A jeep went by and
a loud wolf whistle
arched over the morning,
and hung there,
a tremulant rainbow
into the future.

# *Powder Mitts*

Every year for
my birthday I get
at least three
powder mitts for
after-bath
powdering. A useless
present. I never use
them. They smell
too sweet for me, like
church in wintertime.
I don't want to announce
to the world that I'm coming.
So I have boxes
and boxes of powder mitts
stacked on a bathroom shelf.
One day I took
eight boxes to the backyard.
We each put on a pair like
boxing gloves, they were
stiff and heavy with powder,

and we had a powder-mitt fight.

We were having a fine
old time whacking
each other and making
our own sweet snowstorm
until the powder smell drifted
into the house. My mother
came running out
hollering at us to stop
wasting those perfectly good mitts.
If I'd used one every night
like I was supposed to,
I would have used them up
anyway,
but she didn't
see it that way.
She put the boxes back
on the shelf to multiply
and we retreated
to the scuppernong arbor.

We should have had
the fight at Judy's house.
Her mother wouldn't

have come out, even
if we'd made a real
snowstorm.

# *Why*

Why do we always play
at Judy's house? Is it only
the lure of the green-vined
grape arbor, the glasshouse,
the forbidden garage?
Or is it something more,
the unknown, the unexplained,
the mystery of the cavelike house
and the ghostly mother,
the invisible father?
My father is Norwegian
Judy said. That was how
we knew that
she had one.

# Knowledge

Judy never
came to play at our houses.
We never
told her not to come.
We never
told her to come either.
Our mothers
didn't approve of her mother
they didn't even know.
Somehow,
Judy knew.

# *Our Houses*

Our houses were light
and airy and wore curtains
that breathed in
and out at the windows with
every impulse of breeze.

Our houses wore bright colors
and rang with bright sound,
the cook singing over
the biscuit board, banging
the rolling pin down
on the beat, the radio
droning at noon the "Talk
of the Town" show, our mothers'
voices talking on the telephones,
the rustle of our fathers'
newspapers as they
"kept up with the world."

In our houses
shadows were only
the other sides of things.

# *Our Parents*

Talking was what
our mothers did,
all day, to each other,
to us, to drop-ins, on
the phone. Their shoes
dented the pile in the rugs
when they walked from room
to room and clicked on the bare
wood of the floors between. They
laughed and whistled
and their rings sparkled
in the dishwater.
They hugged us a lot.
Our fathers came home
for lunch everyday
and we could call
them at work on the phone.
They smoked cigars
and slept late on
Sundays and wore

Panama hats to church.
They took us fishing
on their days off
and gave us all
the change in their pockets,
sometimes.

# Growing Crystals

At night
the moonlight shines through
the panes of the greenhouse.
Judy says she can see
it from her window.
It looks like it is filled
with water, she says.
In the morning
the glass crystals
are deeper on the floor.
Does the moonlight
make them grow?

# The Pool

In front of Judy's house
an oval pool was
guarded by a pink plaster flamingo.

Daily it stared
into the green depths
for flashes of goldfish amidst
the tangle of waterweeds
and lily pads.
On hot days the fish
hung motionless in the still
water and the flamingo
glimpsed itself in the mirror
of the pool. Yellow lilies
bloomed like small
fallen suns until
shattered into pieces
of eight by forty
dabbling brown toes.

# The Web

One morning
we found a web
stretched taut
across a windowless pane
in the greenhouse.
A spider had spun it
in the night, a giant
snowflake of spider spit.
It glittered with dew diamonds
and the spider gleamed
like black glass with
red beads on its back
until the sun got high
and we decided it was
a black widow.
They're poisonous
we shouted.

Someone produced a shoe
but the spider was experienced

and escaped through
a crack. The lacy
remnants of web hung
like ragged curtains
all summer.

## Birthday Party

Pinafores and playsuits
in ice-cream colors,
party games on the lawn
under watchful mother eyes.
Judy came in shorts
bearing a large box
wrapped in red
creased Christmas paper
tied with a frayed red bow,
a big shiny apple
amidst the pale pinks
and blues of the other presents.
Open it first
Judy said.
But my mother pushed
another into my hands.
Open this one, she said.
Dutifully, I did.
A Spanish doll ruffled
and flounced stared dumbly

up at me. How nice, she's
very pretty, thanks George, I said.
Embarrassment pinked his face.
His mother picked it out, he
mumbled. George knew
I never played with dolls.

I pushed aside three
obvious powder mitts
but my mother gave me
a look so I opened one,
then passed up a pen
and pencil set, opened
a record, and reached
for the red box. Everyone
crowded closer to see.
I peeled away the wrapping
and opened the box
to find it stuffed with tissue.
Nestled in the middle was
a tiny bottle of nail polish
glowing like a ruby in the sun.

Just what
I wanted, I shouted.

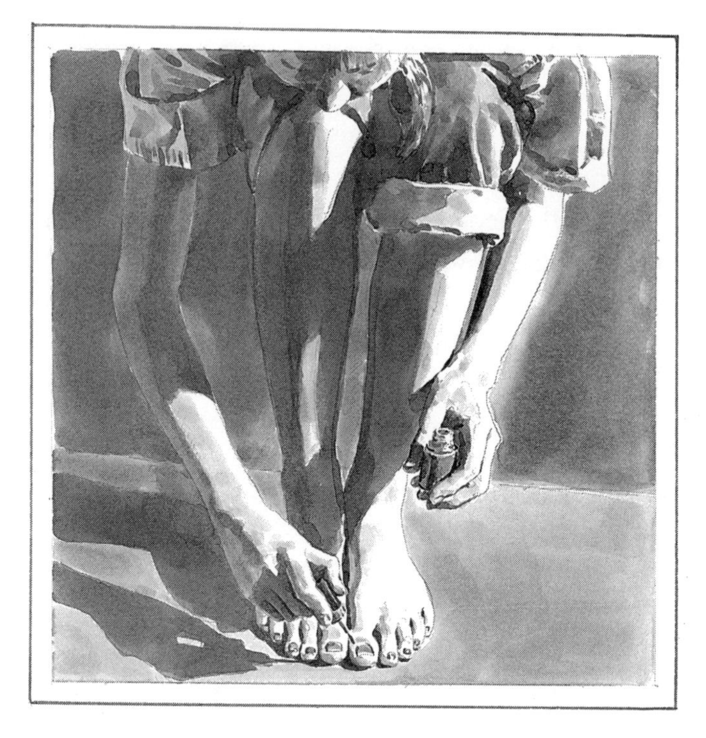

My mother winced
and made me wait
until the party was
over before I could paint
my toenails
Jungle Red.

# Judy's Birthday

Come at one,
Judy said,
in lieu of invitations.
My mother wrapped up
one of the powder mitts.
Out of her sight
I stuck a gold turtle
pin in the middle of
the pink bow. It had green
stones that glittered like
a ring of water around its
shell and ruby eyes with only
one missing. Bill had
traded it for an empty
plasma bottle out of my
father's doctor bag last
year. It still had two eyes
then.

We walked ten blocks

to the Grand Theater.
Judy paid fourteen cents
each to Miss Ida with
a fresh gardenia pinned
to the neck of her white
dotted Swiss blouse, as
she sat on a high stool
alone in her glass booth.

I bet she would use a powder mitt.

Judy bought us each
a nickel Coke and
a nickel candy bar.
Two movies, a serial,
a cartoon, and four previews
later we emerged with newborn
eyes in the late afternoon sun.
Judy had four cents
left so we each
got a gumball from
the newsstand machine
and planned to
explore Africa
all the way home.

# Night Visitors

The crystal dust
grew ankle deep
in the glasshouse.
Maybe it's star
droppings,
or fossilized moonlight,
or bat tears,
we speculated.
Maybe it comes from Mars,
Judy said, brought by
little green men.
We argued awhile
because in that case
shouldn't the dust be green?
Judy agreed to keep
watch one night.
Nobody came, she reported.
And the mystery crystals grew
up to our knees.

# Clues

We crawled through
the azalea tunnel
we'd made between
the bushes and the front
of my house, Stacy and me,
with Indian stealth.
(Lala was at the dentist.)
Our mothers were having
a Grown-Up Conversation
with glasses of Coke
tinkling with ice
and windows as wide open
as our ears. Run
along and play,
our mothers said. We want
to talk. This meant
about things not meant
for our ears. This meant
gossip with neon allure.
We went out the back

door, circled the house,
and took our positions
under the windows. Their
voices drifted out
droning, monotoning,
lifting and dropping,
like boats on a tantalizing sea.
. . . she drinks, you know.

No! How do you . . .
The signs are all there
. . . seen it before . . .
alcoholics . . . poor child . . .
dark rooms . . . neglect . . .
crime . . . shame . . .
Stacy and I looked
at each other. Who
did they mean?

# The Death Marsh

We called it
the Death Marsh because
once we found the bones
of a dog, its brown leather collar
rotting, its tag rusted.
Laddie, we all said.
Laddie had disappeared the fall
before. Our mothers said
he'd probably gone off to die
alone. Dogs do that, they said.
But Laddie wasn't sick.
Maybe he was hit by a car.
Dogs crawl away to die alone
then, too, they said. And
he always ran loose.
That was true.

He chewed off ropes,
slipped out of chain collars,
busted through screens,

dug under pens,
climbed fences,
and opened gates.
Laddie was a dog
that had to be free.

We were sure
those were Laddie's bones
in the marsh so
we buried them there
where he could be free.
We lugged an octagon-shaped
paving stone from Judy's
backyard to mark
his grave and put flowers
on it every time we went,
mostly goldenrod
and other wildflowers
we didn't even know
the names of.

# The Monster

A snapping turtle lived
in the marsh. We never
saw it but we knew
it was there.
Everyone said so.
It was prehistoric,
left over
from dinosaur days.
We walked warily
through watery grass and mud.
It could bite off a foot
or at least a toe.

# *Wood Forts*

There were forts
in the woods behind
Judy's house, mounds
of pine straw built
by boys. If
we heard them
we ran because
they would pelt us with
the spiny pinecones.
They were bigger than we
and could throw the cones
as fast as a baseball
which hurt a lot.
Sometimes
we destroyed one
fort and left others
so they would get blamed.
Sometimes we took
the pinecones out of one
and put them in another.

Then when the war began
and one gang jumped
in its fort,
it would be out
of ammunition.
That was the only way
to get even.

## *Wood Violet*

In
the pine-straw path
untrodden
the bloom
of a single white violet,
a tiny star dropped
from the sky,
one night
gleams alone
in the deep
woods gloom.

# Nobody Cared

if Judy wore shorts
to a birthday party,
went barefoot to town,
painted her toenails Jungle Red.

Nobody cared

if Judy ate cookies for breakfast,
stayed up all night,
washed her hair in the backyard hose.

Nobody cared

if Judy read love comics,
didn't go to Sunday school,
didn't act like a young lady.

Nobody cared.

## *The Bottles*

One day
I went alone
to Judy's house.
The others were having
their eyes tested
and their braces checked.
Judy came out
carrying a grocery bag
full of tall bottles.
They clanked together
without breaking.
The top ones
glistened in the sunlight.
They looked like
they had been washed
clean, inside and out.
Even the labels were gone.
Judy didn't see
me. I stooped
behind a camellia bush

and watched her go
into the greenhouse alone.
Then I heard the sound
of breaking glass
for a long time.
When Judy came out
her eyes were clear
like drops of water.

# Secrets

I never told Judy
I'd seen her. I never
told our mothers they
were right. I never
told Stacy or Lala.
For years we speculated why.
We told fabulous tales
about the magic glasshouse
and passed them down
to younger kids.
But the crystals never grew
after that summer.
The tenth summer moon
is magic, we said.

# The End

We never saw
Judy leave,
never saw her father,
never saw more
than a shadow
of her mother,
never saw a moving truck
or a car leave.
Judy disappeared
like a rainpool
and summer ended.